Katie Blows Her Top

by Fran Manushkin

illustrated by Tammie Lyon

PICTURE WINDOW BOOKS
a capstone imprint

Katie Woo is published by Picture Window Books,
A Capstone Imprint
1710 Roe Crest Drive
North Mankato, Minnesota 56003
www.capstonepub.com

Library of Congress Cataloging-in-Publication Data
Names: Manushkin, Fran, author.
Title: Katie blows her top / by Fran Manushkin.
Description: North Mankato, Minnesota : Picture Window Books/ Capstone Press, [2018] | Series: Katie Woo | Summary: Katie's class is building model volcanoes, but when most of the ingredients end up on Katie, she blows her top.
Identifiers: LCCN 2017031064 (print) | LCCN 2017031880 (ebook) | ISBN 9781515822691 (eBook PDF) | ISBN 9781515822714 (Reflowable Epub) | ISBN 9781515822653 (hardcover) | ISBN 9781515822677 (pbk.)
Subjects: LCSH: Woo, Katie (Fictitious character)—Juvenile fiction. | Chinese Americans—Juvenile fiction. | Science—Experiments—Juvenile fiction. | Elementary schools—Juvenile fiction. | CYAC: Chinese Americans—Fiction. | Science—Experiments—Fiction. | Volcanoes—Fiction. | Schools—Fiction.
Classification: LCC PZ7.M3195 (ebook) | LCC PZ7.M3195 Kal 2018 (print) | DDC 813.54 [E] —dc23
LC record available at https://lccn.loc.gov/2017031064

Graphic Designer: Ted Williams

Printed and bound in the USA.
010765S18

Table of Contents

Chapter 1

A Blast at School

Katie was feeling tip-top.

She told her dad, "Today I'm going to learn about volcanoes. It will be a blast!"

On the way to school, Pedro said, “Volcanoes are awesome! But I don’t want to be near one.”

“I do,” said Katie. “I want to hear the KABOOM!”

Miss Winkle told the class, “When hot melted rock and gas reach the top of the mountain, BOOM! The volcano explodes. It can bury a city!”

"Sometimes we know when a volcano blast is coming," said Miss Winkle. "Sometimes it's a surprise."

"I have a surprise for you," said Miss Winkle. "Today, we are making volcanoes! We will work in teams."

Katie picked JoJo and Pedro.

Miss Winkle gave them some clay and a bottle.

She said, “The first step is to mold this clay around the bottle. Try to make the shape of a mountain.”

Pedro grabbed all the clay and tried to make a mountain.

"Stop!" said Katie. "Our mountain is lumpy!"

"Lumpy is fun," Pedro said.

"No!" said Katie. "Lumpy is wrong!"

"The clay will need time to dry," said Miss Winkle. "We will finish our volcanoes after lunch."

Chapter 2

What a Mess!

During lunch, Katie told Pedro, “Don’t be a volcano hog. I want to do the rest! I know I can make it explode.”

“Hey!” yelled JoJo. “What about me?”

After lunch, Miss Winkle gave each team white vinegar and red food coloring to mix in a bowl.

"Let's make the lava super red," said Katie.

Oops! She poured in too much, and the red spilled on her shirt.

"Yuck!" Katie groaned. "What a mess!"

“The next step,” said Miss Winkle, “is to pour baking soda on a paper towel.”

“I’ll do it,” said Pedro.

“No. Me!” said JoJo.

JoJo tried to grab the baking soda. Oops! The soda went flying and landed on Katie's head!

"Yikes!" yelled JoJo. "You are a mess!"

KABOOM!

That's when Katie blew her top. Her cheeks got hot and red, and she made angry faces.

Boy, did Katie make faces!

"Wow!" said Pedro. "You are fierce! You said you wanted to be close to a volcano. And you are! You became a volcano!"

"I am a volcano?" said Katie. "Wowzee! Sometimes I *am* a little fierce."

"For sure," agreed Miss Winkle. She sent Katie to clean up.

Chapter 3

KABOOM!

Later, JoJo told Katie,

"Let's start a new volcano,

and this time we will be fair.

We will each do our share."

Katie did the last step:

She poured the baking soda

into the bottle.

When it mixed with the

vinegar —

KABOOM!

The lava poured out.

“Wow!” shouted everyone.

“Awesome!”

“High five!” said Katie

and Pedro and JoJo.

After school, Katie said, "Let's be volcanoes all the way home."

Boy, did they yell!

"Kaboom!"

"Kaboom!"

"KABOOOOOM!"

About the Author

Fran Manushkin is the author of many popular picture books, including *Happy in Our Skin*; *Baby, Come Out!*; *Latkes and Applesauce: A Hanukkah Story*; *The Tushy Book*; *Big Girl Panties*; *Big Boy Underpants*; and *Bamboo for Me, Bamboo for You*. There is a real Katie Woo — she's Fran's great-niece — but she never gets in half the trouble of the Katie Woo in the books. Fran writes on her beloved Mac computer in New York City, without the help of her two naughty cats, Chaim and Goldy.

About the Illustrator

Tammie Lyon began her love for drawing at a young age while sitting at the kitchen table with her dad. She continued her love of art and eventually attended the Columbus College of Art and Design, where she earned a bachelor's degree in fine art. After a brief career as a professional ballet dancer, she decided to devote herself full-time to illustration. Today she lives with her husband, Lee, in Cincinnati, Ohio. Her dogs, Gus and Dudley, keep her company as she works in her studio.

Glossary

baking soda (BAYK-ing SOH-duh)—a white powder used in baking to make dough rise

clay (KLAY)—a kind of earth that can be shaped when wet

explode (ek-SPLODE)—to blow apart with a loud bang and great force

fierce (FIHRSS)—daring and dangerous or strong

gas (GASS)—something that is not liquid or solid and does not have a definite shape

lava (LAH-vuh)—the hot, liquid rock that pours out of a volcano when it erupts

melted (MEL-tud)—changed from a solid to a liquid

vinegar (VIN-uh-gur)—a sour liquid, often made from cider, that is used to flavor food

volcano (vol-KAY-noh)—a mountain with openings through which lava, ash, and gas may erupt

Let's Talk

1. Katie picked her friends to be on her team. Is that a good way to pick teams? Why or why not? How do you pick teams?

2. Pedro compared Katie to a volcano. How is Katie like a volcano?

3. Katie's team started over with a new volcano. Compare the second time they built a volcano to the first. What did Katie and her team do differently?

Let's Write

1. Research volcanoes and write a paragraph about what you learned.

2. List the things about Katie's volcano project that made her angry. Then make a list of some times you got angry. What made you feel better?

3. Miss Winkle told the teams each step to make their volcanoes. Using the book as your guide, write down the steps you would need to do to make a volcano. Pretend you are writing these directions to a friend.

Having Fun with Katie Woo!

Katie Woo and her friends built a volcano. They had a blast! Now you can build your own volcano too. Get your friends together to help. Just be sure to share the work!

Exploding Volcano

What you need:

- a big garbage bag
- scissors
- an empty plastic water bottle
- a funnel
- air-dry clay
- an old bowl
- 1 cup of white vinegar
- red food coloring
- 4 tablespoons of baking soda
- a paper towel

What you do:

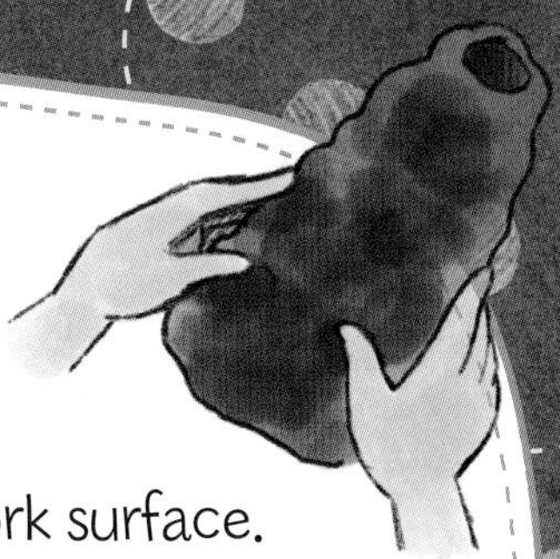

1. Cut open the garbage bag, and spread it out to protect your work surface.

2. Mold the clay around the bottle in a cone shape. Make sure the top of the cone is a little taller than the top of the bottle. Let the clay dry for at least one hour.

3. Pour the vinegar into the old bowl. Add 5 or 6 drops of red food coloring to the vinegar for red "lava."

4. Set the funnel in the top of the plastic bottle inside your volcano. Carefully pour the colored vinegar into the bottle through the funnel.

5. Pour the baking soda onto the paper towel. Then, using the funnel, pour the baking soda from the towel into the vinegar in the plastic bottle.

6. Stand back and watch your volcano explode!

THE FUN DOESN'T STOP HERE!

Discover more at www.capstonekids.com